Yuk!

To Sue Brandon, my fabric guru – KG
To Isabel – NS

YUKI
A RED FOX BOOK 0 099 44804 1

First published in Great Britain by The Bodley Head,
an imprint of Random House Children's Books

The Bodley Head edition published 2004
Red Fox edition published 2005

1 3 5 7 9 10 8 6 4 2

Text copyright © Kes Gray, 2004
Illustrations copyright © Nick Sharratt, 2004

The right of Kes Gray and Nick Sharratt to be identified as the author and illustrator of this
work has been asserted in accordance with the Copyright, Designs and Patents Act 1988.

Set in Lemonade

Red Fox Books are published by Random House Children's Books,
61–63 Uxbridge Road, London W5 5SA,
a division of The Random House Group Ltd,
in Australia by Random House Australia (Pty) Ltd,
20 Alfred Street, Milsons Point, Sydney, NSW 2061, Australia,
in New Zealand by Random House New Zealand Ltd,
18 Poland Road, Glenfield, Auckland 10, New Zealand,
and in South Africa by Random House (Pty) Ltd,
Endulini, 5A Jubilee Road, Parktown 2193, South Africa

THE RANDOM HOUSE GROUP Limited Reg. No. 954009

www.kidsatrandomhouse.co.uk

A CIP catalogue record for this book is available from the British Library.

Printed and bound in Singapore

Yuk!

Kes Gray & Nick Sharratt

RED FOX

Daisy didn't do dresses.

"You can't be a bridesmaid if you won't wear a dress," explained her *mum*.

"Then I won't be a bridesmaid," humpphed Daisy.

Daisy's mum put her arm
around Daisy's shoulder.
"If you don't wear a dress to
Auntie Sue and Clive's wedding,
I'll be sad,
Nanny will be sad,
Grampy will be sad,
Clive will be sad,
everyone in the whole
world will be sad,"
exaggerated Daisy's mum.

Daisy unfolded her arms and sighed.
"I'll wear my football kit!" offered Daisy.

"Bridesmaids don't wear
football kits," sighed Daisy's mum.

"Scuba gear looks good!" offered Daisy.

"Or how about a leopard skin suit?"

"We're going to be in a church, Daisy, not a zoo," sighed Daisy's *mum*.

"At least come and try some dresses on,"
said Auntie Sue.

"Yes," said Daisy's *mum.* "Please come and try some
dresses on. I think *you'd* look lovely in a dress."

Daisy stuck her hands in her pockets and shrugged her shoulders. She didn't do lovely either.

"If I don't like them, I'm not wearing them," she grumbled.

Daisy's mum and Auntie Sue smiled at each other and rushed Daisy to the wedding dress shop before she could change her mind.

Daisy tried the first dress on.

It was passion pink satin with rosebuds and frilly bits.

"Yuk," said Daisy.

Daisy tried the second dress on.

It was yellow silk with sequins and soppy gloves.

"Yuk," said Daisy.

Daisy tried the third dress on.

It was blue velvet with bows and puffy sleeves.

"Yuk," said Daisy.

Daisy tried on every bridesmaid dress in the shop.

But the cotton and the tartan and the organza and the chiffon and the lace and the pleats and the petticoats and the ruffles and the sashes and the embroidery and the appliqué and the ribbons and the tiaras and the handbags and the headdresses were all yuk.

Yuk!

Yuk!

Daisy's *mum* looked at Auntie Sue.

Auntie Sue looked at the dress shop owner.

Everyone had run out of ideas.

Except Daisy.

"I'll tell you what," said Daisy. "I will wear a dress if
I can draw it myself."

Daisy's mum raised her eyebrows and looked at Auntie Sue.

"It's a deal," said Auntie Sue.

When Daisy got home, she ran upstairs and closed her bedroom door. She laid out some big pieces of paper on her bedroom floor and tipped the crayons from her pencil case onto her bed.

When Daisy's *mum* came upstairs to call Daisy to dinner, she found a note pinned to Daisy's bedroom door.

When Daisy's *mum* came upstairs with Daisy's pyjamas she found another note pinned to Daisy's door.

"I do hope it isn't a vampire's dress," sighed Daisy's *mum*.

On the day of the wedding, a smiling Auntie Sue arrived at the church, wearing her wedding dress.

It was white satin with sequins and lacy bows and came with a rosebud tiara.

Behind Auntie Sue came a smiling Daisy,
wearing her bridesmaid's dress.

It was green silk and came with a black ninja headband, *maximum* confetti action belt and hidden extras.

Confety akshun belt

Ninjer hed band

Secrit confety powch

The moment the wedding was over, Daisy reached for her confetti action belt and blammed everybody big time.

She got Auntie Sue down the front of her dress and Uncle Clive down his collar.

She got the Vicar in the ear,

Nanny in the handbag,

and Grampy in the camera.

"How do you like me in a dress?" laughed Daisy, hitting her mum right in the mush with two handfuls.

Daisy's *mum* sighed and began picking bits of confetti out from between her teeth.
"Yuk, Daisy!" she spluttered.

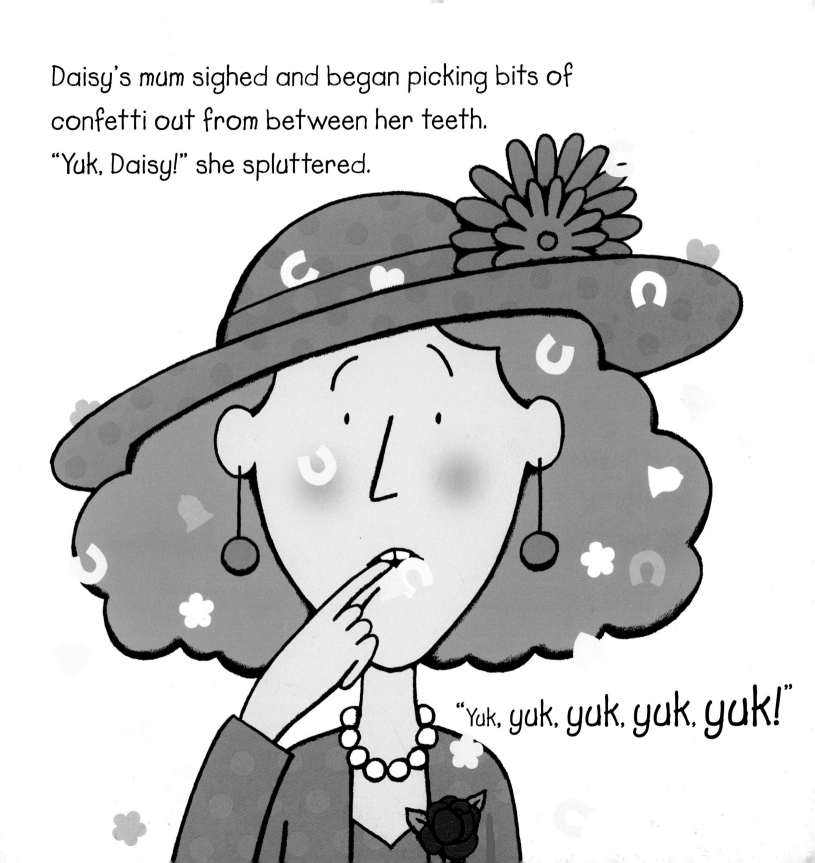

"Yuk, yuk, yuk, yuk, yuk!"

Find out more about Daisy!

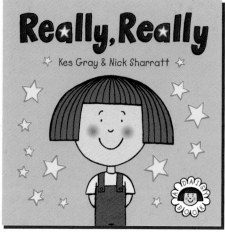

© Daisy has never had a
babysitter before. Will Angela
be fooled by all her fibs?
And will Daisy really, really
get away with them? ©

© Daisy's back bigger than
ever with biscuit problems,
painting lessons, puddle-
jumping, monkey trouble and
a pot of bubbles . . . ©

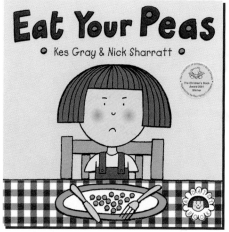

© Mum tries everything to
get Daisy to eat her peas.
But does she eat them, or will
she turn the tables on Mum? ©

Winner of the Children's Book Award • Stockport Schools Book Award for KS1
Sheffield Children's Book Award • Experian Big 3 Award

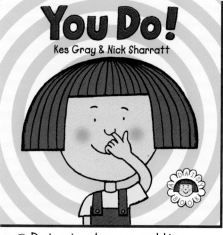

© Daisy is always getting
told off. But she thinks her
mum does just as many
naughty things. Is it true? ©

Come and play with Daisy at www.**kidsatrandomhouse**.co.uk/daisy